D0198702

For Freya, Love from David

To Amy, Love from Stephen

KATE, THE CAT AND THE MOON
by David Almond and Stephen Lambert

British Library Cataloguing in Publication Data
A catalogue record of this book is available from
the British Library.
ISBN 0 340 77386 3 (HB)

First edition published 2004
10 9 8 7 6 5 4 3 2 1

Published by Hodder Children's Books
a division of Hodder Headline Limited
338 Euston Road London NW1 3BH

Originated by Dot Gradations Ltd, UK
Printed in China

Kate, The Cat and The Moon

David Almond and Stephen Lambert

Hodder
Children's
Books

A division of Hodder Headline Limited

Once, in a shining night,
while the moon looked down
and the stars glittered in the endless sky,
and all the house was lost in dreams…

…the little girl called Kate woke up and heard a cat.
"Miaow," called the cat. "Miaooow!"

Moonlight fell across Kate's face.
A million stars glistened in her eyes.
"Miaow," called the cat from the night.
"Miaow. Miaow. Miaow."

Kate tiptoed to the window in her white nightdress.
The cat was on the garden wall.
It licked its paws.
It stretched its neck.
It swung its tail.
Its coat shone, as white as the moon.
It turned its starry eyes to Kate.
"Miaow," Kate whispered. "Miaow. Miaow!"

Kate smiled as she changed.
She touched her pointy ears.
Out of the bedroom, over the landing, down the stairs.

She licked her tiny sharp teeth
with her tiny rough tongue.
She lifted her paw to her face
and felt the whiskers growing there.
She felt her smooth soft coat.
She scratched her claws against the floor.
She licked her paws
and stretched her neck
and swung her tail.
"Miaow," she called. "Miaow!"
And her voice was high and wild
and strange.

She listened.

Grandma snored.

Brother Pete laughed.

Mum and Dad whispered.

The cat called.
And Kate was out in the
shining night.

Through the shadows of the garden,
through the silvery light.
She stopped beneath the garden wall.
Two cats together
in the shining night
as the moon looked down.

Off they went, into the night…

Past dreaming houses, shady gardens,
through pitch-black lanes,
down broad pavements,
under burning street lights,
over empty roads and massive bridges,
past the edge of the town,
through hedges and ditches
and into the fields.
Jump, jump, jump!
To a little hill with a stony top.

"Miaow," they howled.
"Miaoooooooow!!"

The moon looked down.
It licked its tiny sharp teeth
with its tiny rough tongue.
"Miaow," it called. "Miaow!"

And all the sky was full of dreams…

Back through the fields,
the hedges and ditches,
over the bridges and roads and pavements,
back beneath the burning street lights,
through pitch-black lanes,
past dreaming houses and shady gardens
and back to the garden wall.

The stars went out.
"*Miaow,*" said the cat.
"*Miaow,*" said Kate.

Flap, click, clack, stop.
She listened.

Up the stairs, jump, jump, jump!

Across the landing,

into the bedroom,

into bed.

She closed her eyes
and went to sleep...

Next day the talk was all of dreams.
"We walked by Heaven Lake," said Mum and Dad.
"I chased Patch through Butcher Street," said Pete.
"And I danced all night long with Grandpa at the Roxy!"
"Did you dream, Kate?" they asked.

"Miaow," said Kate. *"Miaow."*